PIGGY BUNNY

Story by
RACHEL VAIL

Pictures by
JEREMY TANKARD

FEIWEL AND FRIENDS ○ NEW YORK

To my own sweet Liam
—R. V.

For Theo
—J. T.

A Feiwel and Friends Book
An Imprint of Macmillan

Text copyright © 2012 by Rachel Vail.
Illustrations copyright © 2012 by Jeremy Tankard.
Printed in China by South China Printing Co. Ltd.,
Dongguan City, Guangdong Province.

For information, address Feiwel and Friends, 175 Fifth Avenue, New York, N.Y. 10010.

Library of Congress Cataloging-in-Publication Data
Vail, Rachel.
Piggy Bunny / Rachel Vail, illustrated by Jeremy Tankard. — 1st ed. p. cm.
Summary: Liam is a piglet who wants to be the Easter Bunny when he grows up, but no one believes
he can do it until, with a lot of practice and some help from his grandparents, he shows them all.
ISBN: 978-0-312-64988-3
[1. Individuality—Fiction. 2. Self-confidence—Fiction. 3. Pigs—Fiction. 4. Animals—Infancy—Fiction.
5. Easter Bunny—Fiction.] I. Tankard, Jeremy, ill. II. Title. III. Title: Piggy Bunny.
PZ7.V1916Hel 2012   [E]—dc22   2011001134

The artwork was created with ink and digital media.

Feiwel and Friends logo designed by Filomena Tuosto

First Edition: 2012

1 3 5 7 9 10 8 6 4 2

mackids.com

Liam was just like all the other piglets,
except for one thing.

All the other piglets wanted to be pigs when they grew up.

Liam wanted to be the Easter Bunny.

Liam tried to practice hopping.

He tried to enjoy salad.

And he tried to deliver eggs.

"The Easter Bunny?" asked Liam's big brother. "Seriously?"

"YES," said Liam.

"You are a piglet," said Liam's big sister. "Deal with it."

"I AM dealing with it," said Liam.

Liam was dealing with it by trying to practice hopping.

And trying to enjoy salad.

And trying to deliver eggs.

"You are a terrific piglet," said Liam's mom. "We love your squiggly tail and your little black eyes and your snouty nose and your adorably triangular ears."

"You are perfect," said Liam's dad,
"just exactly the way you are."

"Just exactly the way I am," said Liam, "is like a piglet who is going to be the Easter Bunny."

"Do we even believe in the Easter Bunny?"
asked Liam's little sister.
"Um," said Liam's dad. "We are more
of a believing-in-oinking family."

"I believe in
the Easter Bunny,"
said Liam.

When Liam's grandparents came to visit,
everybody said, "Oink."
"Oink, oink, oink, oink, oink."

Everybody
except
Liam.

Liam said, "Hello, my name is Liam
and I'll be your Easter Bunny."

"Bunny?" asked Liam's grandpa.
"Did this piglet just say he's a bunny?"
"The **Easter** bunny," Liam explained.

"Oh,"

said Grandpa.

"He doesn't look like a bunny to me,"
said one of the neighbors.
All the pigs and piglets stared at Liam.
He didn't look like a bunny to any of them.

"Of course, he doesn't look like
a bunny," said Liam's dad.
"He looks like a perfect piglet."

"And he doesn't have to try to be
anything else," said Liam's mom.
"He's our piglet. And we love him."

Liam felt loved.
But he also felt sad.
Everybody was sure he could
never be the Easter Bunny.
Liam knew they were wrong.
But he wondered a little bit . . .
what if they were right?

Liam sighed.
"This is the kind
of problem,"
he said,
"that is called
heartbreaking."

"Baloney," said Liam's grandma.
"They just have the imagination
of a kumquat, the lot of them."
She shook her large head.
"Go put on your Easter Bunny
suit, Liam. Then they'll see."

Liam blinked his little black eyes.
"But Grandma," he said, "I don't have
an Easter Bunny suit."

Liam's grandpa smiled gently.
"This is the kind of problem," he whispered,
"that is called fixable."
Liam hopped around his grandparents, his
triangular ears twitching with excitement.
"You know how to make an Easter Bunny suit?"
he asked them.

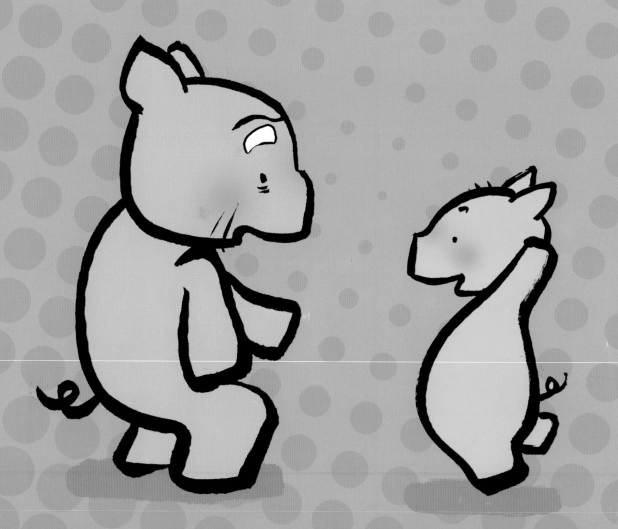

"Absolutely not," said Grandma.
"We will order one on the Internet."

While he waited for his Easter
Bunny suit to arrive,
Liam practiced hopping,

and enjoying salad,

and delivering eggs.
He got pretty good . . .

though salad
remained a
challenge.

When his suit finally arrived, Liam tried it on. It was a bit tight in some places, and way big in others. One of the long bunny ears had trouble standing up straight, even after Grandma fiddled with the wire inside it.

Also, it was
itchy.

Liam looked in the mirror.
He didn't notice the string hanging
down in front of his snout or the wobbly
ear or the too-long sleeves or the seam
coming open a tiny bit across his belly.

He even stopped
noticing the itch.

Because what he saw in the mirror,
looking back at him,
was Liam, the Easter Bunny.

Liam smiled and
whispered, "Yes."

Off he hopped,
delivering eggs.

And everybody believed in him.